THE REAL SCORPION KING

By Cameron Banks

Scholastic Inc.

New York   Toronto   London   Auckland   Sydney
Mexico City   New Delhi   Hong Kong   Buenos Aires

Design by Louise Bova

ISBN 0-439-44062-9

12 11 10 9 8 7 6 5 4 3 2   3 4 5 6 7 8/0

Printed in U.S.A.
First printing, January 2003

This book is based on
The History Channel® special
created by Providence Pictures Inc. Providence,
Rhode Island. With thanks to Gary Glassman,
Executive Producer, Providence Pictures.

Special Thanks to:
John and Deborah Darnell for their
research and photographs used in both
The History Channel® special and this book.

Abbe Raven, Nancy Dubuc and Jim Dowd,
The History Channel®.

Chey Blake and Christina Wright,
A&E Television Networks®.

Contents

PRESENTS

THE REAL
SCORPION KING

By Cameron Banks

Welcome to Ancient Egypt!

Imagine a grand, exotic land where people write in pictures, animals are worshiped as gods, and tombs are the size of palaces. Imagine ancient Egypt!

You probably know that ancient Egypt was a land of pyramids, mummies, and mighty kings. But archaeologists are discovering a treasure trove of surprising facts about the civilization that came *before* the time of the pyramids: the predynastic period. At the center of this older-than-ancient civilization was a powerful, mysterious king whose innovative spirit changed the world. His name? King Scorpion!

Until recently, very little was known about the man who is thought to be Egypt's first ruler. But today, archaeologists from around the world are trekking into Egypt's most desolate deserts, sifting sands for clues, and *wrangling* the world's deadliest creatures to uncover clues from the past.

What they are finding is the truth about a remarkable ruler who is credited with some great inventions. Research tells us that King Scorpion was a key figure in the invention of writing, and his brave actions in battle helped pave the way for a united, stronger Egypt.

Does the name King Scorpion sound familiar to you? That's because this amazing ruler inspired the smash hit Universal Pictures film *The Scorpion King!* In the film, WWE wrestling superstar The Rock portrays the Scorpion King. And The Rock himself hosted the special, *The Real Scorpion King,* which aired on The History Channel® (and on which this book is based!). But a *real* man named King Scorpion did once exist — and we're here to tell you all about him!

Working with The History Channel®, we've traveled the sands of time to search for the man behind the legend. What we've uncovered is an amazing, larger-than-life figure — a pharaoh you won't soon forget. So join us on a journey to the birth of Egyptian civilization, on the quest for the real Scorpion King. . . .

Chapter One

CRACKING THE CODE: TRACKING DOWN KING SCORPION

AN ANCIENT CIVILIZATION

Egypt is so old that it was *ancient* at the time of the Greek and Roman empires! In fact, by the beginning of the Common Era (known as the year one on our modern calendar), the birth of Egyptian civilization was in the distant past.

Much is known about the *end* of the ancient Egyptian empire . . . but little is known about its birth. How *did* one of the greatest civilizations of all time begin? With a great leader, of course!

But the identity of Egypt's first leader remained a mystery for *years* — even to ancient Egyptians.

SPOTLIGHT ON GEOGRAPHY

Long ago, Egypt was divided into two kingdoms: the Upper Kingdom and the Lower Kingdom. The Upper Kingdom was to the south and upstream on the Nile River, and its rulers wore the tall white crown of Upper Egypt. The Lower Kingdom was in the north, where the river delta fans into the Mediterranean Sea. It was controlled by the wearer of the red crown. Egyptian civilization is said to have been born when the two kingdoms were united.

KINGS LIST

To keep track of their rulers, ancient Egyptians created elaborately carved murals on temple walls. As each king took the throne, he would add his name under a picture of the god Horus. Horus was symbolized by a falcon and was thought to be the father of the first human king of Egypt.

The Kings List showed the history of rulers in ancient Egypt, with King Menes as the first king of the first dynasty. Manetho, a priest from ancient Greece, translated the murals' hieroglyphics to write a three-volume history that traced thirty dynasties back three thousand years.

LIFE IN ANCIENT EGYPT
The Last Pharaoh

Most of the rulers, or pharaohs, of ancient Egypt were men. However, the last great pharaoh was a woman — the legendary Cleopatra! Scholars believe that the ancient Egyptian empire began its decline when Cleopatra died at the age of thirty-nine . . . about two thousand years ago!

Did you know . . .

The ancient Greeks gave a name to the ancient Egyptian symbols they saw carved into murals and other places: The Greeks called the symbols *hieroglyphics,* which means "sacred carvings."

But Manetho's original translation was lost. Years later, with the rise of Christianity around 400 C.E., sacred Egyptian writing was banned as devil worship, and soon it was completely forgotten! For more than a thousand years, the history of ancient Egypt and its kings remained a mystery.

CRACKING THE CODE

In 1799, a French soldier in Napoleon's army discovered the Rosetta stone, a large stone tablet with writing in Greek, Demotic (everyday Egyptian script), and ancient Egyptian hieroglyphs (writing used for official and sacred texts). The stone gave very important clues to decoding hieroglyphics — and to Egypt's hidden history.

Scholars rediscovered that King Menes

was the first king of ancient Egypt. But in 1898, two young Egyptologists found an important document now called the Narmer Palette. Narmer, a figure on the palette, was pictured with symbols indicating he was a king — and that he might have unified Egypt. There was just one problem: Narmer didn't appear anywhere on the Kings List! Was the list wrong? Or were the dynasties of Egypt far older than anyone had ever imagined? Archaeologists realized that there may have been kings who came *before* the Kings List. To further complicate

LIFE IN ANCIENT EGYPT
The Secret of the Crowns

One side of the Narmer Palette shows the king wearing the feathered crown of Lower Egypt as he inspects a row of prisoners with their heads cut off. On the other side, he wears the rounded crown of Upper Egypt as he wields a mace (a kind of club) over a kneeling prisoner. These symbolic crowns made scholars believe Narmer brought the two parts of ancient Egypt together.

things, another artifact was found just thirty feet away from the Narmer Palette. The artifact was a large mace head — a kind of weapon used in ancient times. The mace head bore an image of a man facing a scorpion. Who was this new, mysterious figure?

HAIL TO THE KING!

For a long time, very little was known about the mysterious man with the scorpion on the mace head. Was he a mythical figure or an actual ruler? Could he possibly be one of the kings who came before Narmer? Archaeologists guessed that the figure might have represented a king because of the nature of the artifact. Ritual mace heads, or battle clubs, are one of the earliest symbols of kingly power in ancient Egypt. Since kings were often associated with violence and power, they were frequently depicted on carvings as bashing in the heads of their enemies with maces! Mace heads that were used in combat are about the size of baseballs, but ritual mace heads can be the size of basketballs and weigh more than twenty pounds. This mace head with the man and scorpion image is the earliest ceremonial mace head ever found . . . and many thought the mystery man may have been a ruler. Twentieth-century excavations near the remote village of Abydos revealed a vast, amazing underground tomb that offered some more insight into who the "scorpion man" might have been.

FINDINGS AT ABYDOS

The village of Abydos was once one of the holiest places in Egypt. It was said to be the burial site of Osiris, the god of the dead in Egyptian mythology.

For thousands of years, Egyptians came to Abydos to present offerings such as fine wines and oils to Osiris. As a result, in the town, one can find fragments of pots that are more than four thousand years old!

In 1895, a group of excavators dug up nearly 160 tombs in four days. They claimed to find the actual tomb of Osiris — and they fled! But when an English archaeologist named Sir Flinders Petrie arrived on the scene, he rejected the idea that Osiris was buried there. Still, pot fragments and other evidence made him believe that a king from the *prehistory* of Egypt was buried in that spot. But who was this unknown king? Could it be the man on the mace head?

AN UNDERGROUND CRYPT

Fast-forward about one hundred years. In Abydos, archaeologist Dr. Gunter Dreyer picked up where Sir Petrie left off in 1895. In a previously overlooked area, Dr. Dreyer noticed depressions in the ground, which often signify the presence of a tomb.

Dreyer and his team began to dig. They soon came upon a mud brick wall that formed a large chamber. Continuing on, the archaeologists unearthed even more mud brick walls and chambers, finding twelve in all. This huge space was no ordinary tomb!

In fact, it was the largest predynastic tomb ever found. Although the team found no mummy, the tomb contained several hundred artifacts, including non-Egyptian pottery, lots of game pieces, and the ultimate symbol of kingly power: an ivory scepter.

LIFE IN ANCIENT EGYPT
The Stick of Kings!

The scepter that was found in Abydos was shaped like a shepherd's crook. According to archaeologist Dr. Gunter Dreyer, the scepter showed the tomb to be a royal one. He determined that it was the earliest intact scepter ever found in Egypt. Three thousand years after it was made, the scepter is still a symbol of a pharaoh's power!

THE SCORPION CONNECTION

Dr. Dreyer became convinced he had discovered a king from *before* the time of the Kings List. Ink inscriptions on pottery fragments in the tomb featured extraordinary art depicting a scorpion. As Dr. Dreyer says, "From these inscriptions we were finally able to conclude that this tomb belonged to a ruler by the name of Scorpion."

And, naturally, this linked the royal tomb to the mysterious mace head.

Now archaeologists knew for sure that King Scorpion really did exist! But who, exactly, was he? What role did he play in creating one of the greatest civilizations the world has ever known? And why was his symbol . . . a *scorpion*?

Chapter Two

DIGGING DEEPER: DISCOVERING AN INCREDIBLE TOMB

AN AMAZING ARACHNID

Ancient Egyptians worshiped many different kinds of animals. Both gods and human rulers became linked to various creatures. But why would anyone be linked to a scorpion, which is a kind of arachnid? Probably because scorpions are super-tough and very strong survivors. Scorpions, which are a common sight in the Egyptian desert, can live for three months without food or water. They are fast, silent killers — not your ordinary arachnid! (Go to Chapter Four to learn even more about scorpions.)

It's easy, then, to understand why a ruler might want to model himself on this amazing, deadly creature — the ultimate survivor!

PALACE TOMBS

Did you know that the tomb of the Scorpion King was designed to look like his palace? Archaeologists believe that each generation of kings expanded on King Scorpion's basic concept and design for his tomb. Over the centuries, royal tombs slowly evolved into the great pyramids!

Ancient Egyptians believed that when a person died, he or she would go on to an "afterlife." Scientists also claim the huge size of Scorpion's tomb was meant to hold all the *stuff* — from food to perfumes to gold — the ruler would need in the afterlife. Several of these items were thought to have been stolen from King Scorpion's tomb in ancient times.

Other famous tombs, like King Tutankhamen's (known as King Tut), survived for *millennia* without being disturbed. These tombs show the incredible wealth that accompanied the pharaohs in death! Since he was the first to have such an elaborate tomb, the Scorpion King may have set the trend that led to the incredible riches found with King Tut!

THE ART OF MUMMIFICATION

The goal of mummification in ancient Egypt was to preserve the body so that the *ka*, or soul, could reenter the person in the afterlife. During the time of King Scorpion, the art of mummification was just beginning. From the earliest times in ancient Egypt, bodies were wrapped in linen bandages and may have been dried out using salts from the Nile River delta.

As time went on, mummification became very elaborate. Preparing a body turned into a long, involved process that could take up to seventy days!

SPOTLIGHT ON BUILDING

The Scorpion King's tomb is built out of mud bricks — and the same recipe for these bricks is still used today! If you mix earth, straw, and water, drop the mixture into brick forms, and bake it in the sun, you can create the same building material used more than five thousand years ago . . . which has lasted until now! As time went on, buildings for the dead were built aboveground and were made of stone. But the basic construction of tombs evolved from the Scorpion King's simple mud-brick structure.

THE FIRST WRITING?

King Scorpion's architecture for the afterlife wasn't his only contribution to the greatness of Egypt. A discovery in his burial chamber revealed a monumental contribution to civilization. King Scorpion may have been responsible for the first form of *writing* in the world!

TINY TAGS

On the floor of King Scorpion's burial chamber, Dr. Dreyer and his team discovered 160 tiny tags, no bigger than postage stamps, made of bone and ivory. Each of

Did you know...

At over 4,000 miles in length, the Nile is the world's longest river. It flows from south to north, and in ancient times it determined the growing seasons. After the Nile flooded its banks each year, farmers would plant crops in the mud. During the dry season, they would harvest the crops.

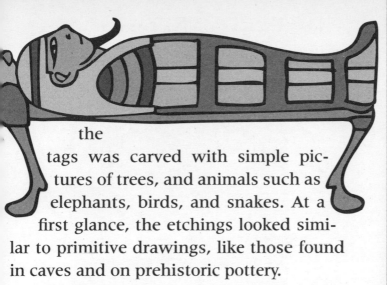

the tags was carved with simple pictures of trees, and animals such as elephants, birds, and snakes. At a first glance, the etchings looked similar to primitive drawings, like those found in caves and on prehistoric pottery.

But these pictures were much more complex than those earlier drawings. Each contained more than one image. For example, one shows a tree and an elephant on mountains. Another shows a tree and a jackal. The images didn't make sense as symbols or as works of art. Did they stand for something else?

SCIENTIFIC TESTING

Mesopotamia, now called Iraq, was thought to be the birthplace of writing. Using carbon dating, Dr. Dreyer discovered that King Scorpion's tags dated back to

3250 B.C.E., two hundred years earlier than writing developed in Mesopotamia!

Some of the pictures on the tags re-

SPOTLIGHT ON SCIENCE

Carbon dating is a scientific way to determine the age of ancient organic items, such as bone and wood. This is the method Dr. Dreyer's team used when investigating the tiny tags.

minded Dr. Dreyer of hieroglyphics, so to "read" the tags, he used phonics from similar hieroglyphics! A tag that showed an elephant on the mountains translated phonetically to the word *Abydos*, which, as you'll recall, is the town where King Scorpion's tomb was found! Other tags translated to other words and places. Dr. Dreyer is convinced that the tags show the world's first writing.

He says, "These labels can be understood only as phonetic writing." What's more, since there isn't evidence of other, more primitive writing, some believe that writing didn't slowly evolve in Egypt. Instead, they think it was invented, practically overnight, because a king demanded it.

TAGS AND TAXES

But why? According to archaeologist Dr. Renee Friedman, the Scorpion King saw the need for writing to keep track of taxes paid — so he ordered his couriers to invent a writing system.

Many of the tags have small holes, and archaeologists believe they were attached to wooden boxes, bolts of linen, and jars of oil that were delivered to King Scorpion as payment from the cities he ruled. The tags were receipts for paid taxes!

Taxes made the kingdom rich. But with wealth and power came rivalries . . . and battles to determine the supreme ruler. These battles would pave the way for a united, stronger Egypt!

EGYPTOLOGY POP QUIZ

Ancient Egyptians invented eyeliner, the 365-day calendar, and toilet seats.
True or false?

(Answer: True)

Welcome to Egypt! These are the famous pyramids of Giza. It is believed that the Scorpion King's lavish tomb was the inspiration for what would become the incredible pyramids.

THE HISTORY CHANNEL®

Discovered in 1799, the Rosetta stone is a stone tablet with writing in Greek, Demotic, and ancient Egyptian. This important discovery helped "crack the code" of Egyptian hieroglyphics (see next photo).

THE ROSETTA

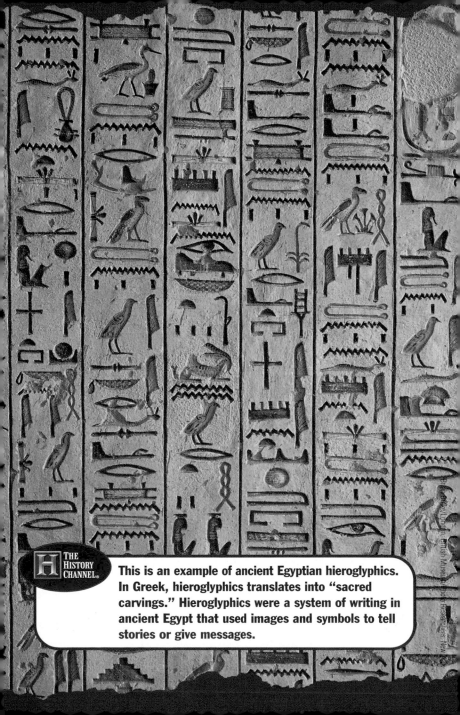

This is an example of ancient Egyptian hieroglyphics. In Greek, hieroglyphics translates into "sacred carvings." Hieroglyphics were a system of writing in ancient Egypt that used images and symbols to tell stories or give messages.

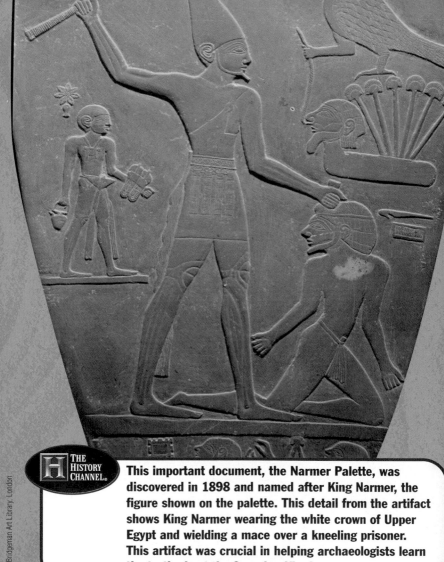

THE HISTORY CHANNEL®

This important document, the Narmer Palette, was discovered in 1898 and named after King Narmer, the figure shown on the palette. This detail from the artifact shows King Narmer wearing the white crown of Upper Egypt and wielding a mace over a kneeling prisoner. This artifact was crucial in helping archaeologists learn the truth about the Scorpion King!

 THE HISTORY CHANNEL® This is a coffin (called a sarcophagus) inside the famous tomb of King Tutankhamen (King Tut). Discovered in 1922, the tomb showed how many fancy treasures ancient Egyptian kings were buried with.

THE HISTORY CHANNEL

The beautiful Nile River in Egypt is 4,665 miles in length—making it the world's longest river. The Nile was a very important part of life in ancient Egypt . . . and it's still a much-visited site today!

Hans Namuth/Photo Researchers, New York

This is a very important detail from the lower portion of the Scorpion Tableau, discovered by John and Deborah Darnell of Yale University. The Darnells interpreted this image to be a faint carving of a primitive scorpion. Combining this with the image on the upper half of the tableau (which shows the falcon symbol of Horus, or "King") the researchers were able to guess that this tableau represented "King Scorpion"!

Does this image look a lot like a real scorpion to you? (see next photo)

THE HISTORY CHANNEL

This is a common Egyptian desert scorpion. Scorpions are amazing creatures with strong survival skills. It's no wonder a king would want to model himself after one. Even though they're superstrong, the creepy-crawlies are still pretty ugly, aren't they?

Courtesy of Serge Mallet.

Chapter Three

SCORPION KING, RULER OF EGYPT

UNITE . . . AND CONQUER!

How did the Scorpion King conquer Upper Egypt? The recent discovery of some amazing artifacts shows that the great leader may have had strong ties to both Abydos in the north and the city of Hierakonpolis in the south.

King Scorpion's connections to both cities, combined with brilliant military strategy, might have enabled him to become the first leader *ever* to unite ancient Egypt.

THE SCORPION TABLEAU

In 1995, Yale University Egyptologist John Darnell discovered a remarkable carving at Gebel Tjauti. The etching, called the Scorpion Tableau, may unlock the mysteries of King Scorpion's rise to power and could prove to be the earliest historic document in Egypt . . . and, possibly, the world!

The five-thousand-year-old carving shows a faint drawing of what looks to be a scorpion. Above this drawing is an image of a falcon, which represents the god Horus. According to Dr. Darnell, these carvings are remarkable because they mark the first

SPOTLIGHT ON GEOGRAPHY

Gebel Tjauti is found on one of the ancient routes connecting Egypt's Qena Bend with the Western Desert, halfway between Abydos and Hierakonpolis. Its central location made it a strategic military site. But thousands of years ago, it was also a very popular destination for picnics!

time that the name of the god Horus is used as a royal title. As Dr. Darnell says, "[It] appears to tell us that the author of these events is a man named Scorpion, or Horus Scorpion."

TRIUMPH OVER ENEMIES

The Scorpion Tableau didn't just show that Scorpion was a king. It also showed him triumphing over enemies.

Part of the tableau shows a prisoner with wild hair, his arms bound by a rope, who is held in the hands of a large figure. The large figure threatens the prisoner with a mace.

LIFE IN ANCIENT EGYPT

The Royal Horus

The Horus name is another word for king, and the title identifies Scorpion with Horus the hawk or falcon, the god of Egyptian kings. The Horus name continued to be used by every Egyptian king for thousands of years . . . but Scorpion was the first king in Egyptian history to use the Horus title!

And who is the large figure that stands victorious over his enemy? Horus Scorpion!

AN HISTORICAL RECORD?

But who was the Scorpion King's prisoner in the image? Behind the captive appears a bull's head on a vertical pole. Dr. Darnell believes that the man's name — "Bull's Head on a Stick" — may be that of the leader of Naqada, a rival ancient city.

Remember Narmer's Palette, the carving showing that Egyptian kings may have existed before the Kings List — and that documents an actual military victory? The Scorpion Tableau has a similar theme — and is thought to be two hundred years older. The Scorpion Tableau may be

Did you know...

Located near Gebel Tjauti, Naqada was where important trade routes came together in ancient Egypt. Whoever controlled those trade routes commanded the wealth of Upper Egypt.

the first known historical document in the world.

HOMETOWN HERO OF HIERAKONPOLIS

Archaeologists believe that Horus Scorpion may have come from Hierakonpolis, the largest city in ancient Egypt. Many artifacts bearing a scorpion symbol were found there, and research suggests that King Scorpion's tomb in Abydos may have been modeled on a palace in Hierakonpolis. With ties to both Hierakonpolis and Abydos in 3250 B.C.E., King Scorpion would have been the right man at the right time to lead a united force against the armies of Naqada.

ATTACK!

How did the Scorpion King lead the battle against Naqada? Dr. John Darnell believes that he launched a sneak attack, beginning in the deserts of Gebel Tjauti. By hiding out behind a mountain in a desert pass known as the Narrow Door, the Scorpion King could wait with his army — and attack the Naqada army at just the right moment.

By marching through the desert, the Scorpion King could completely avoid the large Naqada army in the Nile Valley. Then, driving rapidly north, King Scorpion's troops from Abydos could cut off Naqada forces.

It's thought that King Scorpion commanded a quick and relatively bloodless victory over Naqada.

VICTORY . . . AND KICKOFF TO HISTORY!

Experts believe that King Scorpion may

EGYPTOLOGY POP QUIZ

In 3,000 B.C.E., each Egyptian family made their own bread at home. True or false?

(Answer: False. Industrial-size bakeries started producing bread, which was used as money at that time.)

LIFE IN ANCIENT EGYPT
A Cosmic Battle?

Hierakonpolis and Abydos both share the patron deity Horus, the falcon god who sprang forth from Osiris. The patron god of Naqada is Set, the god of chaos — and enemy of Osiris. The battle between the Scorpion King's army and Naqada might also have been a kind of cosmic battle — between opposing gods of chaos and order. In ancient rock art, the people of Naqada are depicted as wild, feather-wearing hunters and warriors — as opposed to the more "civilized" Scorpion King.

have paraded the captured Naqada ruler back to Abydos — and marked the occasion by ordering the carving of the Scorpion Tableau.

The event signified the start of the unification of Upper and Lower Egypt, a long process that involved diplomacy, trade, commerce, and sharing technology. Some experts believe that King Scorpion was at the heart of the origins of a culture that would continue to develop for millennia!

SCORPION KING, GREAT LEADER

Experts believe that after the Naqada battles, King Scorpion went on to rule a rich kingdom. He developed trade routes as far away as Afghanistan, used writing to keep track of his riches and art to celebrate the power of the gods — and his own triumphs.

The Scorpion King built palaces and temples for the living and tombs for the dead. As depicted on some works of art, he may have even brought water to his land and wealth to his people. He set the stage for an enduring belief in the central importance of the king for running the government.

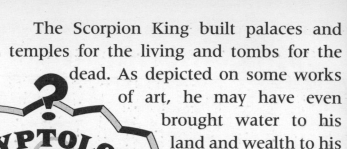

EGYPTOLOGY POP QUIZ

Because his accomplishments were so great, some experts believe that the Scorpion King may actually have been two different people! True or false?

(Answer: True)

ONGOING EXCAVATIONS

While the legendary Scorpion King and his accomplishments have come to light in recent years, much still remains unknown. Archaeologists continue to try to solve the mysteries and piece together the history of the entire predynastic period.

While many events and details surrounding the Scorpion King are still a mystery, one thing is certain: He was *real*. His accomplishments are key to the great civilization of ancient Egypt. And his legacy of culture, art, architecture, military skill, and more will live on . . . forever!

Chapter Four

SCORPIONS, SCARABS, AND OTHER CREATURES OF ANCIENT EGYPT

THE ANIMAL-HUMAN CONNECTION

The Scorpion King was named for one of the toughest and deadliest members of the arachnid family. Like many rulers who followed him, he was associated with a particular animal, and writings about the Scorpion King featured a trademark picture of the desert creature. (It made him easy to remember!)

While they connected leaders to powerful creatures, ancient Egyptians also worshiped certain animals. That's because Egyptian gods and goddesses were connected to specific animals — and were believed to appear as those creatures. Ancient Egyptians worshiped falcons and hawks (like Horus, the royal bird-god, who was said to be the father of all human rulers), jackals, dogs, fish, crocodiles, snakes, hippos, dogs, cats, and even *bugs*!

SACRED SCARABS

The scarab beetle was common in ancient Egypt and was prized as a symbol of immortality. But why?

Scarab beetles lay their eggs in dung, where they are protected from predators. (And believe it or not, scarab beetles eat dung, so it is a food source for them as well.) The ancient Egyptians were amazed by beetles that seemed to magically grow out of, well, waste.

When making a mummy, embalmers would place a scarab amulet over a person's heart. The

EGYPTOLOGY POP QUIZ

Many families in ancient Egypt had pet monkeys or birds, along with the usual cats and dogs. True or false?

(Answer: True)

amulet symbolized the worth of a person — and was thought to be an important part of gaining entrance to the afterlife.

CELEBRATED CATS

Cats were some of the most treasured animals in ancient Egypt. Cats were so important, in fact, that it was against the law to kill a feline!

Cats were associated with the goddess Bastet, who was linked to good fortune and health. Ancient Egyptians believed that every cat carried Bastet's power with them and brought good luck. Cats were so highly prized that many, many feline statues were buried with people, to accompany them to the next life.

On a practical level, cats were important in ancient Egypt because they protected people — and their food! Cats eat rodents that can spread disease and eat grain. Keeping cats as pets was a very important way to control rats and mice and to safeguard food for humans.

PET CEMETERIES

From the time of the Scorpion King, Egyptians honored the falcon Horus, patron of kings. But did you know that Egyptians also paid tribute to animal gods by burying *mummies of animals* in special cemeteries?

The cat god Bastet is honored at Bubastis, where people left mummified felines in large numbers! In other places, the faithful offered dogs in honor of the jackal-headed god Anubis and fish to Osiris (who was eaten by fish).

LIFE IN ANCIENT EGYPT
Animal Oracles?

Sacred animals were kept in temples, in the shrines of their patron gods. There, they would answer questions from the faithful! For example, if a creature ate from one bowl of food, it meant the answer to a question was yes, and eating from another meant no. Like other oracles, these special animals were believed to be able to tell the future.

Thoth, the god of wisdom and writing, has the head of an ibis, a large bird. Thoth was an important god and was frequently honored. In fact, one ancient Egyptian cult cemetery honoring Thoth is said to contain *four million* ibis mummies!

SCORPION KING: THE ORIGINAL "SPIDER-MAN"!

The kings of ancient Egypt were closely linked to the gods. In fact, they were thought to be direct descendants of animal gods!

The traits of an animal that represented a human ruler may tell us about the ruler himself. What was King Scorpion *really* like? We might be able to tell something simply by looking at scorpions — the creepy-crawly kind!

Scientists estimate that scorpions have been around for about 420 million years — which means these creatures are pretty tough. And scorpions have changed very little over the years. In fact, a scorpion you see today might look similar to a scorpion that lived millions of years ago!

There are more than fifteen hundred species of scorpions, and some of them have been given names such as "emperor scorpion" and "death stalker." (Yikes!) The scientific name for the common Egyptian scorpion is *Androctonus australis*, or "southern man killer." This kind of scorpion — which King Scorpion named himself after — is indeed a very fast and silent killer. The creature carries a very powerful venom — a kind of poison — that it uses to defend itself against a would-be attacker. A scorpion's sting is *very* dangerous . . . and can be deadly. Of the fifteen hundred known species of scorpion, twenty can kill humans with their sting. So if you happen to run into a scorpion . . . stay far away!

SCORPION SURVIVOR

Besides turning nasty when threatened, scorpions also know how to take very good care of themselves. Desert conditions — intense heat and dryness — are often rough on living beings, but scorpions have a special chemical in their skin that helps them retain moisture even under the scorching desert sun. But when it gets cold, scorpions can still survive. These creatures can endure extreme changes in tempera- ture. Amazingly, scor- pions can be frozen in a block of ice — and still be in fine shape! Scorpions can also sustain themselves for *three months* without any food or water. These arachnids may be small — but they're superstrong.

Now that you know about some of their incredible features, it's easy to understand why a long-ago king — who needed to be tough — would want to model himself after scorpions. With potent venom, great speed, and astonishing survival skills, scorpions are strong and simply awe-inspiring . . . just like the human ruler who called himself King Scorpion!

STILL CURIOUS? CHECK OUT . . .

From the development of writing to the ancient blueprints of incredible pyramids, the Scorpion King and his era are where it all began in ancient Egypt. Studying this great ruler and his contributions to culture and society is a fun way to learn about a history that goes back *more than* 5,000 years, to practically the birth date of Western civilization!

If you liked reading about the Scorpion King, you'll love learning more about the legends and lives of other people in ancient Egypt! And what better place to start than with some cool motion picture entertainment? These films don't offer factual accounts of life in ancient Egypt, but they're fun stories about mummies, magic, and one particular king who just *may* be pretty familiar to you!

Did you know...

- The word *pharaoh* comes from the words *per aa*, which, in Egyptian, meant "a palace or great house where the ruler lived."

- In ancient Egypt, boys' heads were shaved, leaving just one braid. (Not exactly a popular hairstyle today!)

- Ancient Egyptians did not use forks, knives, or spoons. They ate meat with their hands.

- Doctors who diagnosed problems, created medicines, and performed operations were common in ancient Egypt. There were even medical schools at temples to train people.

MUMMY CLASSICS

People have been fascinated by ancient Egypt for a long time. And one of the most interesting aspects of that ancient civilization was its mummies! Mummy mania really got going in the 1920s, when King Tutankhamen's tomb was discovered in Egypt. By the 1930s, the first mummy movie had hit the silver screen.

The Mummy (Universal Pictures, 1932) stars Boris Karloff as an Egyptian prince named Imhotep who falls in love with a princess. When the princess dies, Imhotep tries to raise her from the dead — a forbidden act. Imhotep is caught and punished by being buried alive. Many years later, he reemerges . . . as a creepy mummy!

In *The Mummy's Tomb* (Universal Pictures, 1942), a high priest travels to the United States with Kharis, a living mummy, to seek revenge on those who destroyed the tomb of an Egyptian princess. The film is the first of a three-part series about the mummy Kharis and stars the famed Lon Chaney Jr.

MODERN MUMMY MOVIES

Like the first *Mummy* movie from 1932, *The Mummy* (Universal Pictures, 1999) is

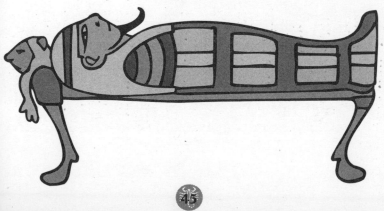

an exciting story about a powerful, scary mummy coming to life! But this smash hit film, starring Brendan Fraser, is an original adventure not based on previous *Mummy* movies.

In *The Mummy Returns* (Universal Pictures, 2001) it's back to ancient Egypt for an action-packed sequel, once again starring Brendan Fraser. This movie features The Rock as a man named Mathayus, who is based upon King Scorpion!

In *The Scorpion King* (Universal Pictures, 2002), a modern prequel to the two *Mummy* movies, The Rock returns to the big screen to do battle in the ancient Egyptian desert! The film draws upon the legend of the real Scorpion King that you may know just a *few* things about now!

Here's the story as it's shown on film: Mathayus, played by The Rock, is asked by nomadic, or wandering, tribes to lead the battle against a wicked warlord named

Memnon. The evil Memnon and a beautiful sorceress plan to conquer all the desert tribes. It's up to Mathayus to unite the tribes — and save the people from danger. The movie about this brave ruler is fun and fast-paced entertainment. But for the *real* facts on the *real* King Scorpion, you may want to stick to the info in this book . . . or investigate some other cool sources (see next page!).

LIFE IN ANCIENT EGYPT

"Old" School?

Several thousand years ago, Egyptian kids went to school, just like kids today! Between the ages of four and fourteen, they learned to read, write, and do mathematics. They also played games, learned to swim, and wrestled!

EGYPT ONLINE . . .
AND ON TV

Dying to know more about mummies, pyramids, hieroglyphics, and other wonders of ancient Egypt? Hoping to learn more about the facts behind the legends? Then check out *www.HistoryChannel.com*. The History Channel store (at *ShopHistoryChannel.com*) has tons of special programs on ancient Egypt that are sure to grab your attention. Some programs you might enjoy include:

- *Egypt Beyond the Pyramids*
- *Mummies and the Wonders of Ancient Egypt*
- *Great Builders of Egypt*
- *Egypt: Land of the Gods*
- *The Great Pharaohs of Egypt*

And, of course, the video and program that this book is based on — *The Real Scorpion King*.

Also, remember to visit your local library or museum — they're sure to have lots of resources to keep you interested . . . and learning more!

THE REAL SCORPION KING:
The Ultimate Challenge

You've discovered the secrets of the Scorpion King! How about testing your "Egyptology Quotient," and seeing how much you re-member about the amaz-ing ancient world?

1. The god Bastet appears as a
   a. fish
   b. cat
   c. jackal

2. The Scorpion Tableau shows the king
   a. triumphing over his enemies
   b. eating and drinking
   c. inventing writing

3. In Greek, the word *hieroglyphics* means
   a. picture writings
   b. animal art
   c. sacred carvings

4. The scarab beetle was common in ancient Egypt and was prized as a symbol of
   a. strength
   b. love
   c. immortality

5. The Nile River is the world's
   a. deepest river
   b. longest river
   c. widest river

6. How long can a scorpion survive without food or water?
   a. three months
   b. nine months
   c. three years

7. The tiny tags found on the floor of the Scorpion King's burial chamber were believed to be
   a. ancient postage stamps
   b. ancient game pieces
   c. ancient tax receipts

8. In Egyptian mythology, Osiris is god of the
   a. dead
   b. hunt
   c. harvest

9. In 3500 B.C.E., the largest city in Egypt was:
   a. Abydos
   b. Hierakonpolis
   c. Cairo

10. Who found the Rosetta stone in 1799?
    a. a French soldier
    b. the Scorpion King
    c. Cleopatra

GLOSSARY

Archaeologist (ark-ee-AH-lo-gist): a scientist who studies ancient civilizations through their artifacts.

Artifacts (ART-i-fakts): objects from the past.

Commerce (CAHM-ers): exchange of goods or property between nations or individuals.

Diplomacy (dih-PLOH-muh-see): the art and practice of negotiations between nations.

Dynasty (DIE-nuh-stee): generations of rulers who belong to the same family; the period of time that family reigned. (In ancient Egypt, *predynastic* means the time before dynasties were recorded.)

Egyptology (EE-jihp-TAH-luh-gee): the study of the language, history, culture, and civilization of ancient Egypt. (An *Egyptologist* is an expert in or student of Egyptology.)

Millennium, millennia (plural) (muh-LEH-nee-um): a period of one thousand years.

Oracle (OR-uh-kul): a place, thing, or person said, in ancient times, to deliver messages from gods.

Phonics (FAH-niks): sounds that symbolize written characters or letters.

Receipt (ree-SEET): a written acknowledgment that something, such as money or goods, has been received.

Resin (REH-suhn): a solid substance formed from the sap of various plants or trees used to seal materials.

Scepter (SEHP-ter): a staff or rod carried by royal figures as a sign of authority.

Trade (TRAYD): the business of buying and selling; an exchange of one thing for another.